For Jessica, Jane and Toby

Copyright © 1995 by Jane Chapman. All rights reserved. No part
of this book may be copied or reproduced in any form without
written permission from the publisher.
All trademarks are the property of
Western Publishing Company, Inc.,
Racine, Wisconsin 53404.
ISBN: 0-307-17570-7   A MCMXCV

First published 1995 in Great Britain by
ABC, All Books for Children, a division of
The All Children's Company, Ltd.

Library of Congress Cataloging-in-Publication Data

Chapman, Jane.
Mary's baby / written & illustrated by Jane Chapman.
p.   cm.
Summary: Mary and Joseph travel to Bethlehem, where the baby
Jesus is born in a stable because there is no room in the inn.
1. Jesus Christ—Nativity—Juvenile literature. [1. Jesus Christ—
Nativity. 2. Bible stories—N.T.] I. Title.
BT315.2.C46   1995
232.92—dc20   95-5524
CIP   AC

Printed in Singapore

Mary's Baby

By Jane Chapman

ARTISTS & WRITERS GUILD BOOKS
Golden Books®
Western Publishing Company, Inc.
850 Third Avenue, New York, N.Y. 10022

Mary's Baby was coming.
An angel had come to see her.
"Don't be afraid. The Baby
is coming and all will be
well," he told her.

Mary and Joseph went to Bethlehem. "Oh, Joseph, the Baby is coming!" Mary said.

It was night in Bethlehem and every inn was full.
"I need a room," Joseph said to everyone.
But there was no room.
"The Baby is coming," he said loudly.

The innkeeper came to the door.
"The Baby is coming?" he asked.
"Go to the stable, quick."

"The Baby is coming," whispered Mary.

In the fields an angel visited the shepherds. "The Baby is coming," he told them.

Three wise men saw a beautiful star.
"You know what that means," they
said to each other. "The Baby is coming."

The shepherds came down from the fields.

The wise men traveled from far away.

The innkeeper's wif
came to the stable.

The angels sang.

"The Baby Jesus is here," they said.